DISCARD

MATH IN OUR WORLD

EXPLORING
SOLID FIGURES
ON THE WEB

By Linda Bussell

Reading consultant: Susan Nations, M.Ed.,
author/literacy coach/consultant in literacy development
Math consultant: Rhea Stewart, M.A., mathematics content specialist

WEEKLY READER®
PUBLISHING

Please visit our web site at www.garethstevens.com
For a free color catalog describing our list of high-quality books,
call 1-800-542-2595 (USA) or 1-800-387-3178 (Canada). Our fax: 1-877-542-2596

Library of Congress Cataloging-in-Publication Data
Bussell, Linda.
    Exploring solid figures on the web / by Linda Bussell.
      p. cm. — (Math in our world level 3)
    Includes bibliographical references and index.
    ISBN-10: 0-8368-9287-9 — ISBN-13: 978-0-8368-9287-1 (lib. bdg.)
    ISBN-10: 0-8368-9386-7 — ISBN-13: 978-0-8368-9386-1 (softcover)
      1. Geometry, Solid—Juvenile literature. 2. Geometry, Descriptive—Juvenile literature.
  3. Web sites—Design—Juvenile literature. I. Title.
  QA491.B86 2008
  516.23—dc22   2008012125

This edition first published in 2009 by
Weekly Reader® Books
An Imprint of Gareth Stevens Publishing
1 Reader's Digest Road
Pleasantville, NY 10570-7000 USA

Copyright © 2009 by Gareth Stevens, Inc.

Creative Director: Lisa Donovan
Designer: Amelia Favazza, *Studio Montage*
Copy Editor: Susan Labella
Photo Researcher: Kim Babbitt

Photo Credits: cover, title page: Corbis; p. 4: Hemera Technologies; p. 5: Tony Freeman/ Photo Edit; p. 6: Mary Kate Denny/Photo Edit; pp. 7, 18: Photodisc; p. 8: David Pollack/Corbis; p. 10: Discovery Science Center; p. 12: Kazuyoshi Nomachi/Corbis; p. 13: Richard Nowitz/Corbis; p. 14: Corbis; p. 15: Patrick Ward/Corbis; p. 17: Jonathan Bailey Associates; p. 19: Staud/www.phototravels.net; p. 20: Frans Lemmens/Getty Images

All rights reserved. No part of this book may be reproduced, stored in a retrieval system, or transmitted in any form or by any means, electronic, mechanical, photocopying, recording, or otherwise, without the prior written permission of the copyright holder.

Printed in the United States

1 2 3 4 5 6 7 8 9 10 09 08

Table of Contents

Chapter 1: Sights for a Site 4

Chapter 2: Places With Faces 7

Chapter 3: Odd Shapes and Round Shapes 13

Chapter 4: Open House 16

What Did You Learn? 22

Glossary 23

Index 24

Words that appear in the glossary are printed in **boldface** type the first time they occur in the text.

Chapter 1

Sights for a Site

The students at King School return from school break. They gather near the library before computer club. They talk about what they did on the break.

Emily says, "I visited my grandmother." She shares a postcard of the city where her grandmother lives. "There is a building shaped like a pyramid in the city," says Emily.

Other students look at the picture. Tamara says she has seen a picture of a building shaped like a **sphere**. Terrell has seen a building that looks like a **cube**.

The class decides to make a web site about buildings shaped like geometric solids.

Terrell has an idea. "We can make a web site for our computer club project," he says. "It can be about buildings that are shaped like geometric solids." The students agree. They think that it will be a fun project.

"First we must find pictures of buildings," says Antonio. "Then we can build our web site."

"Let's ask the librarian and the computer teacher for help," says Emily. The children enter the school library and the computer lab.

They visit the librarian, Mr. Bowen. They explain their idea for the project. "This will be an interesting project," says Mr. Bowen. "I will help you find books you might need."

They visit the computer teacher, Miss Washington. "I will help you design your web site," says Miss Washington. "I will help you with Internet research, too."

The students want to use photos on their web site. Miss Washington says, "You must give credit to the photographer when you use pictures that are not yours."

These students are doing research to find buildings shaped like geometric solids.

Chapter 2

Places With Faces

With the help of Mr. Bowen and Miss Washington, the students find lots of information. Then they talk about how to make the web site.

"We should work in pairs," says Antonio. "It will make the project go faster."

"That is a good idea," says Tamara. "Each pair should find a picture and information. They can share the information with the group."

"Each pair can learn about a different solid," says Robert. "Then we will build our web site."

Ana and Terrell work together. They want to find a picture and information about a solid figure. They talk about **rectangular prisms**.

"Rectangular prisms are solid figures," Ana says. "They have six faces that are all rectangles."

Terrell looks at a web site on the computer. "Many office buildings are shaped like rectangular prisms," he says.

Miss Washington helps Ana and Terrell. They search for pictures of buildings. They find pictures of many office buildings. Most of the buildings are shaped like rectangular prisms.

This is the United Nations building in New York City.

Antonio and Nicole look for pictures of buildings shaped like cubes. "Cubes are a special kind of rectangular prism," says Antonio. "Cubes have six square faces."

Nicole says, "All the square faces of a cube are exactly the same."

Miss Washington helps Antonio and Nicole search the Internet. They search for "cube buildings." They find a building in California that looks like a cube.

"The cube is 10 stories tall," Antonio says. "One face of the cube is covered with 464 solar panels. The solar panels turn sunlight into energy."

This is the Discovery Science Center in Santa Ana, California.

Emily and Jessica study pyramids. "A **square pyramid** has a base that is a square," Emily says. "Its four triangle-shaped faces all meet at one common point. The base is a face, too."

"Can we find a picture of the Great Pyramids?" asks Jessica. "They are in Egypt."

Mr. Bowen helps them find a picture of the Great Pyramids. They find it in a book about Egypt. "The Pyramids are very old," says Jessica. "They were built more than 4,500 years ago."

These are the Great Pyramids in Giza, Egypt.

Chapter 3

Odd Shapes and Round Shapes

Some solids have curved surfaces. Anthony and Robert learn about spheres.

"Spheres are solids that are round," says Anthony. "A sphere is shaped like a ball."

"Every point on the curved surface of a sphere is the same distance from the center," says Robert.

Mr. Bowen points out that buildings usually are not true spheres. A sphere would only touch the ground at one point. Anthony finds a picture of a structure that looks like a sphere.

This is Spaceship Earth at Disney's Epcot in Orlando, Florida.

Erin and Kai learn about **cylinders**. "Cylinders are solids that look like cans," says Kai. "Two faces on a cylinder are shaped like circles."

Miss Washington helps them find pictures of buildings that look like cylinders. "Some water towers are shaped like cylinders," says Erin.

Erin and Kai also look for buildings shaped like **cones**. They do not find any. Miss Washington suggests they look for buildings that have parts shaped like cones. She offers to help them with their search.

These cylinder-shaped buildings are in Los Angeles, California.

A cone is a solid, pointed figure. It has a flat, round base. It has one curved surface. Miss Washington finds a picture of a castle. The castle has a tower. The tower has a cone-shaped top. Erin and Kai plan to make a web page for buildings that have cone shapes.

"Some buildings are made of different solid shapes put together," says Miss Washington.

"Let's find other buildings that have more than one shape," says Erin.

"We can make a web page of buildings with combined shapes," says Kai.

The towers of the castle have cone-shaped tops.

Chapter 4

Open House

    The students finish their research about solid figures. Miss Washington helps them build their web pages. Then the students help Erin and Kai. They find many buildings made of more than one solid figure.

    They add more web pages to display the pictures they find. These are the most interesting pages of all! Finally, the students finish their project. They complete their web site about buildings shaped like solid figures.

    They are pleased. The web site has turned out very well. The students plan to show it during Open House.

The Winnie Palmer Hospital in Orlando, Florida, has buildings with several solid figures.

On the night of the Open House, parents, teachers, and students visit the library. They come to see the web site that the students in the computer club created. People gather around to see the final project.

The students talk about their web site. Each visitor has a favorite web page. Everyone likes the pictures of complex solids. Those web pages show buildings that combine two or more solid figures.

One web page shows an office building. The students point out some of the solid figures for their visitors. "Look at this building," says Terrell. "Here is a rectangular prism."

"This building looks like it has many rectangular prisms," says Nicole. "I wish I could walk around it and see the other sides. This part is shaped like a cube."

Soon, visitors take turns trying to name the solids they find.

Part of this office building in Vienna, Austria, is cube-shaped.

The students share another web page. The top of one building is made of a row of cubes. Each cube points toward the sky.

"I wonder what it would be like to walk around inside this building," says Kai. "How would they hang pictures on the wall?"

"The computer club has done an excellent job," says Mr. Bowen.

"You have learned many things about solids," says Miss Washington.

The visitors congratulate the students. The club members smile. Everyone had fun.

These cube-shaped apartments are in Amsterdam, Netherlands.

What Did You Learn?

① How many faces are found in 3 rectangular prisms, 2 cubes, 2 cylinders, and 4 square pyramids?

② Look around the place where you live. What solid figures can you find? What are they?

Use a separate piece of paper.

Glossary

cone: a solid, pointed figure that has a flat, round base

cube: a solid figure with six congruent square faces

cylinder: a solid or hollow object that is shaped like a can

rectangular prism: a solid figure with six faces that are all rectangles

sphere: a solid figure that has the shape of a round ball

square pyramid: a solid figure with a flat, square base and four triangular-shaped faces that meet at one common point

Index

base 12, 15
cone 14, 15
cube 4, 11, 19, 21
cylinder 14

pyramid 4, 12
rectangular prism 9, 11, 19
sphere 4, 13

About the Author

Linda Bussell has written and designed books, supplemental learning materials, educational games, and software programs for children and young adults. She lives with her family in San Diego, California.

Millbury Public Library

12/08

Millbury Public Library